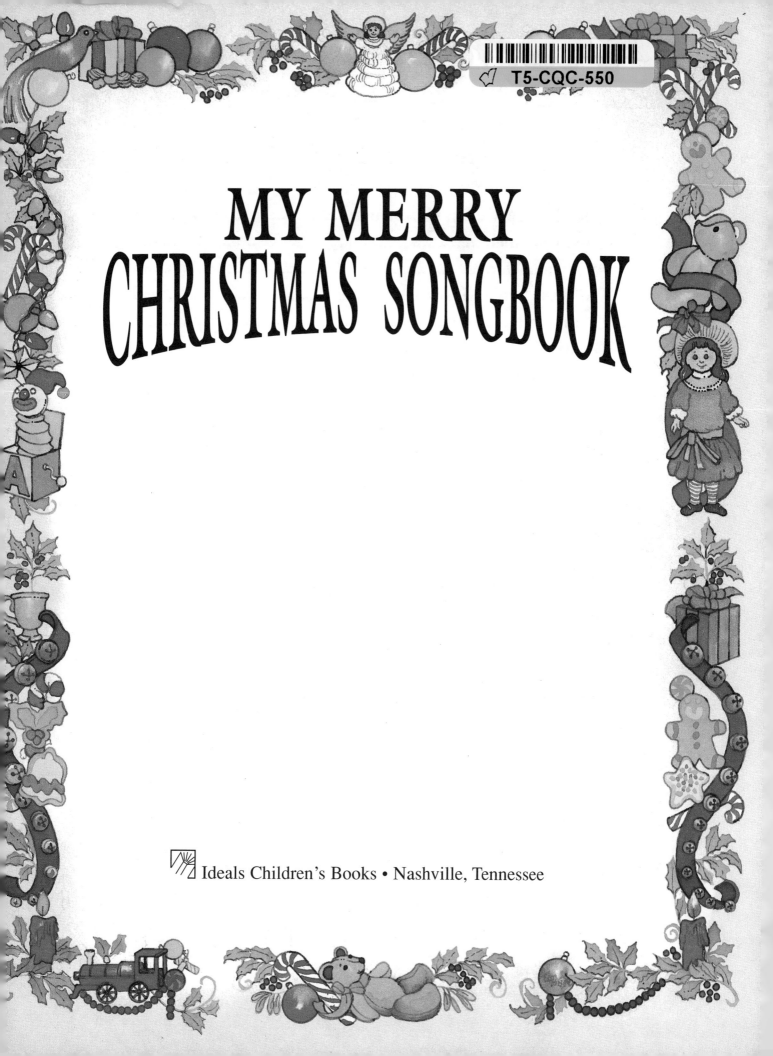

MY MERRY
CHRISTMAS SONGBOOK

Ideals Children's Books • Nashville, Tennessee

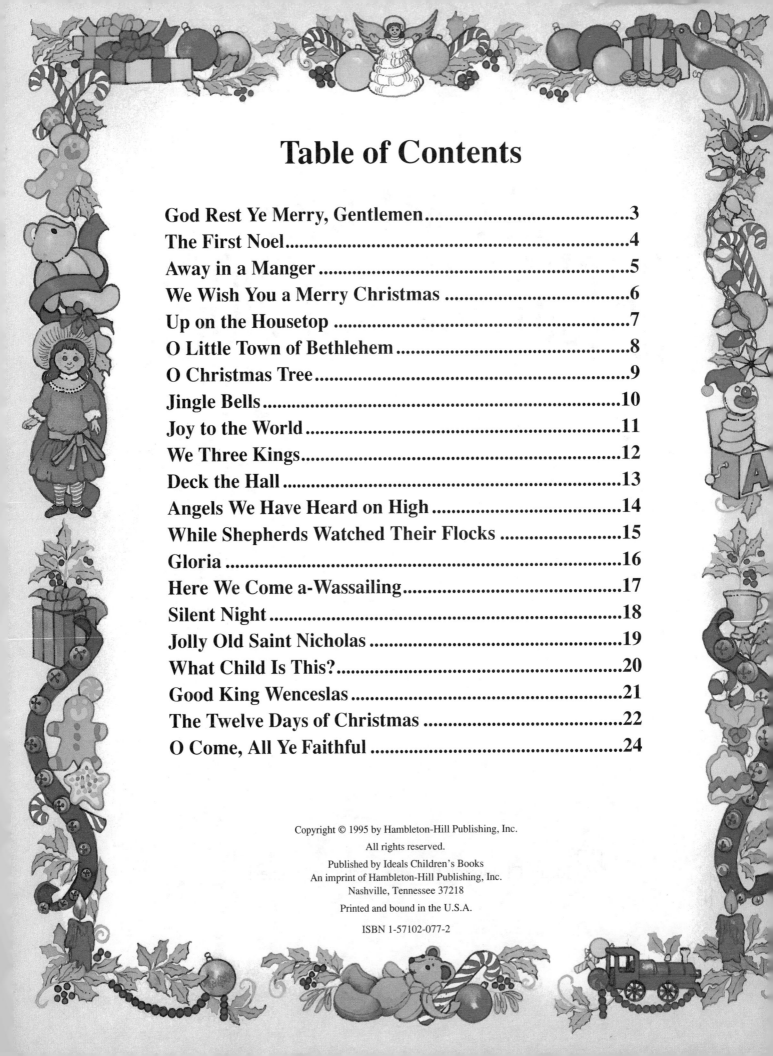

Table of Contents

Copyright © 1995 by Hambleton-Hill Publishing, Inc.

All rights reserved.

Published by Ideals Children's Books
An imprint of Hambleton-Hill Publishing, Inc.
Nashville, Tennessee 37218

Printed and bound in the U.S.A.

ISBN 1-57102-077-2

God Rest Ye Merry, Gentlemen

TRADITIONAL

ENGLISH CAROL

1. God rest ye mer - ry, gen - tle - men, Let noth - ing you dis - may,
2. In Beth - le - hem, in Jew - ry, This bless - ed babe was born,
3. From God our heav'n - ly Fa - ther, A bless - ed an - gel came;
4. Now to the Lord sing prais - es All you with - in this place;

Re - mem - ber Christ, our Sav - ior Was born on Christ - mas Day;
And laid with - in a man - ger Up - on this bless - ed morn;
And un - to cer - tain shep - herds Brought tid - ings of the same;
And with true love and broth - er - hood Each oth - er now em - brace;

To save us all from Sa - tan's pow'r When we were gone a - stray.
The which his Moth - er Ma - ry Did noth - ing take in scorn.
How that in Beth - le - hem was born The Son of God by name.
This ho - ly tide of Christ - mas All oth - er doth de - face.

O___ ti - dings of com____ fort and joy, com - fort and

joy; O___ ti - dings of com - fort and joy.

The First Noel

TRADITIONAL

FRENCH CAROL

1. The first No - el the an - gel did say Was to
2. They look - ed up and saw a star Shin-ing
3. And by the light of that same star, Three
4. This star drew nigh to the north - west, O'er
5. Then en - tered in those wise men three, Full

cer - tain poor shep - herds in fields as they lay; In fields where they lay
in the east, be - yond them far; And to the earth it
wise men came from coun - try far; To seek for a king was
Beth - le - hem it took its rest; And there it did both
rev - 'rent - ly up - on their knee; And of - fered there in

keep-ing their sheep On a cold win-ter's night that was so deep.
gave great light, And so it con - tin-ued both day and night.
their in - tent, And to fol - low the star wher - ev - er it went.
stop and stay Right o - ver the place where Je - sus lay.
his pres - ence, Their gold and myrrh and frank - in - cense.

No - el, no - el, No - el, no - el. Born is the King of Is - ra - el.

Away in a Manger

MARTIN LUTHER   GERMAN CAROL

1. A - way   in a   man - ger,   no   crib   for   His
2. The   cat - tle   are   low - ing,   the   ba - by   a -

bed,   The   lit - tle   Lord   Je - sus   laid   down   his   sweet
wakes,   But   lit - tle   Lord   Je - sus,   no   cry - ing   he

head.   The   stars   in   the   sky——   looked   down   where   he
makes;   I   love   thee   Lord   Je - sus,   look   down   from   the

lay;   The   lit - tle   Lord   Je - sus   a - sleep   on   the   hay.
sky,   And   stay   by   my   cra - dle   till   morn - ing   is   nigh.

We Wish You A Merry Christmas

TRADITIONAL

1. We wish you a Mer-ry Christ-mas, We wish you a Mer-ry Christ-mas,
2. Please bring us some fig-gy pud-ding, Please bring us some fig-gy pud-ding,
3. We won't go un-til we get some, We won't go un-til we get some,
4. We wish you a Mer-ry Christ-mas, We wish you a Mer-ry Christ-mas,

We wish you a Mer-ry Christ-mas And a Hap-py New Year!
Please bring us some fig-gy pud-ding, Please bring it right here!
We won't go un-til we get some, Please bring it right here!
We wish you a Mer-ry Christ-mas, And a Hap-py New Year!

Refrain

Glad tid-ings we bring To you and your kin;

Glad tid-ings for Christ-mas And a Hap-py New Year!

Up on the Housetop

BENJAMIN R. HANBY

1. Up on the house - top__ rein - deer pause,
2. First comes the stock - ing of lit - tle Nell,
3. Next comes the stock - ing of lit - tle Will,

Out jumps good old__ San - ta Claus;
Oh, dear San - ta__ fill it well;
Oh, just see what a glo - rious fill;

Down through the chim - ney with lots of toys,
Give her a dol - ly that laughs and cries,
Here is a ham - mer and lots of tacks,

All for the lit - tle ones' Christ - mas joys!
One that will o - pen and shut her eyes!
Al - so a ball__ and whip that cracks.

Ho! Ho! Ho! Who would-n't go? Ho! Ho! Ho!

Who would-n't go?__ Up on the house - top; Click! Click! Click!

Down through the chim - ney with good Saint Nick!

O Little Town of Bethlehem

PHILLIPS BROOKS

LEWIS H. REDNER

1. O lit-tle town of Beth-le-hem, How still we see thee lie;
2. For Christ is born of Mar - y; And gath-ered all a-bove,
3. How si-lent-ly, how si-lent-ly, The won-drous gift is giv'n!
4. O ho-ly child of Beth-le-hem, De-scend to us, we pray;

A - bove thy deep and dream-less sleep The si-lent stars go by;
While mor-tals sleep, the an-gels keep Their watch of won-d'ring love.
So God im-parts to hu-man hearts The bless-ings of His heav'n.
Cast out our sin and en-ter in, Be born in us to - day.

Yet in thy dark streets shin-eth The ev-er-last-ing light;
O morn-ing stars, to-geth-er, Pro-claim the ho-ly birth;
No ear may hear his com-ing, But in this world of sin,
We hear the Christ-mas an-gels The great glad ti-dings tell;

The hopes and fears of all the years Are met in thee to-night.
And prais-es sing to God, our king, And peace to men on earth.
Where meek souls will re-ceive him still, The dear Christ en-ters in.
O come to us, a-bide with us, Our Lord Em-man-u-el.

O Christmas Tree

Translated from German:
O TANNENBAUM!

GERMAN CAROL

1. O Christ - mas tree, O Christ - mas tree, O tree of green un -
2. O Christ - mas tree, O Christ - mas tree, You set my heart a -
3. O Christ - mas tree, O Christ - mas tree, You come from God, e -
4. O Christ - mas tree, O Christ - mas tree, You speak of God, un -

chang-ing O chang-ing. Your boughs so green in sum-mer-time,
sing-ing. O sing-ing. Like lit-tle stars, your can-dles bright
ter-nal. O ter-nal. A sym-bol of the Lord of love
chang-ing. O chang-ing. You tell us all to faith-ful be,

They brave the snow of win-ter-time; O Christ - mas tree, O
Sent to the world a won-drous light. O Christ - mas tree, O
Whom God to man sent from a-bove. O Christ - mas tree, O
And trust in God e - ter-nal-ly. O Christ - mas tree, O

Christ - mas tree, O tree of green un - chang-ing.
Christ - mas tree, You set my heart a - sing-ing.
Christ - mas tree, You come from God, e - ter-nal.
Christ - mas tree, You speak of God, un - chang-ing.

Jingle Bells

JOHN PIERPONT

Joy to the World

ISAAC WATTS

GEORGE F. HANDEL

1. Joy to the world! the Lord is come! Let earth re-
2. Joy to the world! the Sav - ior reigns; Let men their
3. No more let sins and sor - rows grow, Nor thorns in - the
4. He rules the world with truth and grace And makes the

ceive her King;_____ Let ev - 'ry heart_____ pre -
songs em - ploy;_____ While fields_____ and_____ floods,_____ rocks
fest the ground;_____ He comes to_____ make_____ his
na - tions prove_____ The glo - ries_____ of_____ his

pare him room,_____ And heav'n and na - ture sing, And__
hills,__ and__ plains_____ Re - peat the sound - ing__ joy, Re -
bless - ings__ flow_____ Far as the curse is__ found, Far__
right - eous - ness_____ And won - ders of his__ love, And__

And   heav'n and na - ture

heav'n and na - ture__ sing,   And__ heav'n,__ and heav'n__ and na - ture sing.
peat the sound - ing__ joy,   Re - peat,_____ re - peat - the sound - ing joy.
as   the curse is__ found,   Far as,_____ far as_____ the curse is found.
won - ders of his__ love,   And__ won - ders, and won - ders of his love.

sing,   And heav'n and na - ture   sing.

We Three Kings

JOHN H. HOPKINS, JR.

1. We three kings of O - ri - ent are, Bear - ing gifts we trav-erse a - far,
2. Born a king on Beth - le-hem's plain, Gold we bring to crown him a-gain;
3. Frank-in-cense to of - fer have I, In-cense owns a de - i - ty nigh;
4. Myrrh is mine; its bit - ter per - fume Breathes a life of gath-er-ing gloom;
5. Glo - r'ous now be - hold Him a - rise: King and God and sac - ri - fice;

Field and foun - tain, moor and moun - tain, Fol - low - ing yon - der star.
King for - ev - er, ceas - ing nev - er, O - ver us all to reign.
Pray'r and prais - ing, all men rais - ing, Wor - ship God on high.
Sor - r'wing, sigh - ing, bleed - ing, dy - ing, Sealed in the stone-cold tomb.
Heav'n sing "Hal - le - lu - jah!" "Hal - le - lu - jah!" earth re - plies.

O star of won - der, star of night, Star with roy - al beau - ty bright;

West - ward lead - ing, still pro - ceed - ing, Guide us to thy per - fect light.

Deck the Hall

TRADITIONAL   WELSH CAROL

1. Deck the hall with boughs of hol-ly, Fa la la la la, la la la la.
2. See the blaz-ing yule be-fore us, Fa la la la la, la la la la.
3. Fast a-way the old year pass-es, Fa la la la la, la la la la.

'Tis the sea-son to be jol-ly, Fa la la la la, la la la la.
Strike the harp and join the cho-rus, Fa la la la la, la la la la.
Hail the new, ye lads and lass-es, Fa la la la la, la la la la.

Don we now our gay ap-par-el, Fa la la la la la la la la.
Fol-low me in mer-ry meas-ure, Fa la la la la la la la la la.
Sing we joy-ous all to-geth-er, Fa la la la la la la la la la.

Troll the an-cient Yule-tide car-ol, Fa la la la la, la la la la.
While I tell of Yule-tide treas-ure, Fa la la la la, la la la la.
Heed-less of the wind and weath-er, Fa la la la la, la la la la.

Angels We Have Heard on High

TRADITIONAL   FRENCH CAROL

1. An - gels we have heard on high, Sweet - ly sing - ing o'er the plains;
2. Shepherds, why this ju - bi - lee? Why your joy - ous songs pro - long?
3. Come to Beth - le - hem and see Him whose birth the an - gels sing;

And the moun - tains in re - ply Ech - o - ing their joy - ous strains.
What the glad - some ti - dings be, Which in - spire your heav'n - ly song?
Come, a - dore on bend - ed knee Christ, the Lord, our new - born king!

Glo - ri - a

in ex - cel - sis De - o. Glo -

ri - a in ex - cel - sis De - o!

While Shepherds Watched Their Flocks

NAHUM TATE   HUGH WILSON

1.While shep-herds watched their flocks by night, All seat-ed on the ground,
2."All glo-ry be to God on high, And on the earth be peace:

The an-gel of the Lord came down, And glo-ry shone a-round.
Good-will hence-forth from heav'n to men Be-gin and nev-er cease."

"Fear not," said he (for might-y dread Had seized their trou-bled mind);

"Glad ti-dings of great joy I bring, To you and all man-kind."

Gloria

TRADITIONAL

OLD ENGLISH CAROL

1. When the crim-son sun is set   Low be-hind the   win-try sea,
2. Shep-herds watch-ing by their fold,   On the crisp and   hoar-y plain,

On   the bright and   cold mid-night   Bursts a sound of   heav'n-ly glee:
In   the sky bright hosts es-py,   Sing-ing in   a   glad-some strain:

Glo - - - ri - a

in ex-cel-sis De - o;   Glo - - -

ri - a   in ex-cel-sis   De - o.

Here We Come a-Wassailing

TRADITIONAL

ENGLISH CAROL

1. Here we come a-was-sail-ing A-mong the leaves so
2. We are not dai-ly beg-gars That beg from door to
3. Good mas-ter and mis-tress, As you sit by the
4. God bless the mas-ter of this house, Like-wise the mis-tress,

green;— Here we come a-wand'ring, So fair to be seen.
door;— But we are neigh-bor's chil-dren, Whom you have seen be-fore.
fire,— Pray think of us poor chil-dren, Who wan-der in the mire.
too,— And all the lit-tle chil-dren, That round the ta-ble go.

Love and joy come to you, And to you your was-sail

too, And God bless you and send you a hap-py new

year, And God send you a hap-py new year.

Silent Night

JOSEPH MOHR

FRANZ GRÜBER

1. Si - lent night! Ho - ly night! All is calm,
2. Si - lent night! Ho - ly night! Shep - herds quake
3. Si - lent night! Ho - ly night! Son of God,

all is bright Round yon vir - gin moth - er and child,
at the sight; Glo - ries stream from heav - en a - far,
love's pure light, Ra - diant beams from thy ho - ly face

Ho - ly in - fant, so ten - der and mild; Sleep in heav - en - ly
Heav'n - ly hosts sing, "Al - le - lu - ia! Christ, the Sav - ior is
With the dawn of re - deem - ing grace; Je - sus, Lord, at thy

peace, Sleep in heav - en - ly peace.
born! Christ, the Sav - ior is born!"
birth, Je - sus, Lord, at thy birth.

Jolly Old Saint Nicholas

1. Jol - ly old Saint   Ni - cho - las,   Lean your ear this   way!
2. When the clock is   strik - ing twelve, When I'm fast a - sleep,
3. John - ny wants a   pair of skates; Su - sy wants a   sled;

Don't you tell a   sin - gle soul   What I'm going to   say;
Down the chim - ney broad and black, With your pack you'll creep;
Nel - lie wants a   pic - ture book;   Yel - low, blue and   red;

Christ - mas Eve is   com - ing soon, Now, you dear old   man,
All the stock - ings you will find Hang - ing in a   row;
Now I think I'll   leave to you   What to give the   rest;

Whis - per what you'll bring to me, Tell me if you   can.
Mine will be the   short - est one, You'll be sure to   know.
Choose for me, dear   San - ta Claus, You will know the   best.

What Child Is This?

WILLIAM C. DIX

ENGLISH MELODY

1. What Child is this, Who laid to rest On Mary's lap is sleeping?
2. Why lies He in such mean es-tate, Where ox and ass are feed-ing?
3. So bring Him in-cense, gold and myrrh, Come peas-ant, king to own Him;

Whom an-gels greet with an-thems sweet While shep-herds watch are keep-ing?
Good Chris-tian, fear, for sin-ners here The si-lent Word is plead-ing.
The King of kings sal-va-tion brings; Let lov-ing hearts en-throne Him.

This, this is Christ, the King Whom shep-herds guard and an-gels sing!
Nail, spear shall pierce Him through, The cross be borne for me, for you;
Raise, raise the song on high, The vir-gin sings her lul-la-by;

Haste, haste to bring Him laud, The Babe, the Son of Ma - ry!
Hail, hail the Word made flesh, The Babe, the Son of Ma - ry!
Joy, joy for Christ is born, The Babe, the Son of Ma - ry!

Good King Wenceslas

JOHN NEAL

TRADITIONAL

1. Good King Wen - ces - las looked out On the feast of Ste - phen,
2. "Hith - er, page, and stand by me, If thou know'st it, tell - ing,
3. "Bring me flesh and bring me wine, Bring me pine - logs hith - er;
4. "Sire, the night is dark - er now, And the wind blows strong - er;
5. In his mas - ter's steps he trod, Where the snow lay dint - ed;

When the snow lay round a - bout Deep, and crisp and e - ven;
Yon - der peas - ant, who is he? Where and what his dwell - ing?"
Thou and I will see him dine When we bear them thith - er."
Fails my heart I know not how, I can go no long - er."
Heat was in the ver - y sod Which the saint had print - ed;

Bright - ly shone the moon that night, Tho' the frost was cru - el,
"Sire, he lives a good league hence, Un - der neath the moun - tain;
Page and mon - arch, forth they went, Forth they went to - geth - er,
"Mark my foot - steps, my good page, Tread thou in them bold - ly,
There - fore Christ - tian men, be sure, Wealth or rank pos - sess - ing,

When a poor man came in sight, Gath - 'ring win - ter fu - el.
Right a - gainst the for - est fence, By St. Ag - nes' foun - tain."
Thro' the rude wind's wild la - ment, And the bit - ter weath - er.
Thou shall find the win - ter's rage Freeze thy blood less cold - ly.
Ye who now will bless the poor, shall your - selves find bless - ing.

The Twelve Days of Christmas

1. On the first day of Christ-mas my true love gave to me:

a par-tridge in a pear tree. 2. On the
(3. On the)
(4. On the)

sec-ond day of Christ-mas my true love gave to me:
third___ day of Christ-mas my true love gave to me: three French___ hens
fourth___ day of Christ-mas my true love gave to me: four call-ing birds

two tur-tle doves, and a par-tridge___ in a pear tree. 3. On the
4. On the

tree. 5. On the fifth day of Christ-mas my true love gave to me:

five gold___ rings! four___ call-ing birds, three French hens,

FINE

two___ tur-tle doves, and a par-tridge___ in a pear tree.

6. On the sixth___ day of Christ - mas my
7. On the sev - enth day of Christ - mas my
8. On the eighth___ day of Christ - mas my
9. On the ninth___ day of Christ - mas my
10. On the tenth___ day of Christ - mas my
11. On the ele - venth day of Christ - mas my
12. On the twelfth___ day of Christ - mas my

D.S.

true love gave to me: six___ geese a lay - ing,
true love gave to me: sev - en swans a swim - ming,
true love gave to me: eight___ maids a milk - ing,
true love gave to me: nine___ lad - ies danc - ing,
true love gave to me: ten___ lords a leap - ing,
true love gave to me: ele - ven pip - ers pip - ing,
true love gave to me: twelve___ drum - mers drum - ming,

O Come, All Ye Faithful

LATIN HYMN
Translated by FREDERICK OAKELEY

JOHN FRANCIS WADE

1. O come, all ye faith-ful, joy-ful and tri-um-phant;
2. Sing, choirs of an-gels, sing in ex-ul-ta-tion;
3. Yea, Lord, we greet Thee, born this hap-py morn-ing;

Come ye, O come ye to Beth-le-hem;
Sing all ye cit-i-zens of heav'n a-bove;
Je-sus, to Thee be all glo-ry giv'n;

Come and be-hold Him, born the King of an-gels:
Glo-ry to God, all glo-ry in the high-est:
Word of the Fa-ther, now in flesh ap-pear-ing;

O come, let us a-dore Him, O come, let us a-dore Him, O

come, let us a-dore Him, Christ, the Lord.